Love You
Hoo

For my beautiful River . . . Love you hoo

First American Edition 2017
Kane Miller, A Division of EDC Publishing

First published in Great Britain in hardback in 2017 by
The Watts Publishing Group
First published in paperback in 2017

For information contact:
Kane Miller, A Division of EDC Publishing
PO Box 470663
Tulsa, OK 74147-0663
www.kanemiller.com
www.edcpub.com
www.usbornebooksandmore.com

Library of Congress Control Number: 2016955647

Printed in China
2 3 4 5 6 7 8 9 10

ISBN: 978-1-61067-621-2

Love You
Hoo
Kane Miller
A DIVISION OF EDC PUBLISHING

Cuddle up now, little one,
Let's snuggle wing to wing.
Are you feeling safe and warm?
OK then, let's begin ...

There's something I MUST tell you
Before you close your eyes.
I want to
Woo-hoo-hoo it

So it fills the starry skies.

Ever since you hatched, you see,
You set my world alight!
With you - hoo-hoo,

Each day becomes
So colorful and bright.

You make life feel like sunshine,
No matter what the weather.

And ANYTHING is possible,
As long as we're together.

5 STAGE FLYING PLAN
1.
FLAP VIGOROUSLY
2
LEAN IN
CLOSE EYES
JUMP
FLY
I BELIEVE I CAN FLY
GETTING MORE HEIGHT

I'll show you what I've come to know,
And try to teach you things.
Perhaps I'll give a gentle nudge
To help you find your wings.

EMERGENCY
JUST-IN-CASE
PARACHUTE

But . . . you teach me too,
hoo-hoo.
To look through different eyes.
Yes, little ones can often be
So very, VERY wise.

We'll never stop exploring,
There's so much to see and do.
Now you're here, there's **ALWAYS** more
I'm looking forward to.

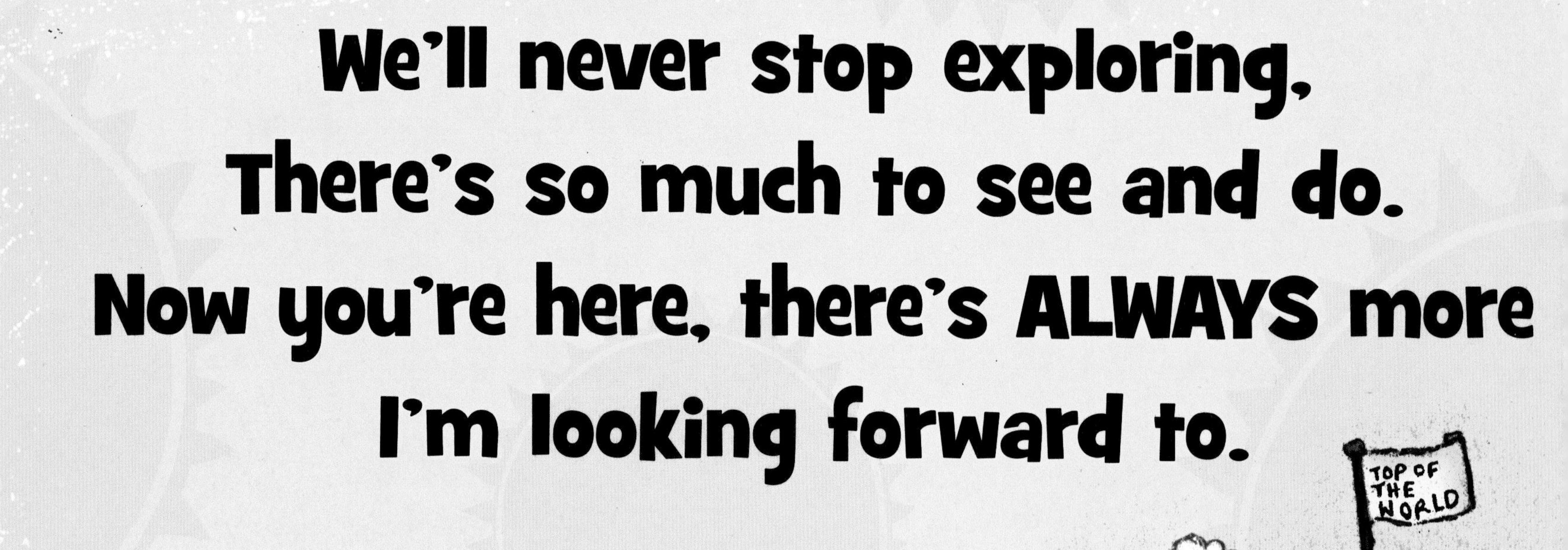

UPS & DOWNS
WONDERFUL ADVENTURES
EMERGENCY JUST-IN-CASE PARACHUTE
GREAT VIEW
GOING WITH THE FLOW
COOL STUFF

And if things don't
quite go to plan,

If there are scrapes ...

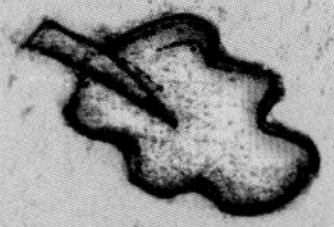

FLYERS
BEWARE
OF
TREE
or BUMPS ...

... we'll cheer ourselves
back up again.
We'll laugh away
the grumps!

Oh, with you life is SO wonderful.
You're times-a-million GREAT!
And everything's a piece of cake,
Whatever's on our plate!

So here are all my kisses,
And another one for sure.
Some hugs and tickles too,

hoo-hoo.

And, then,
perhaps some ...

... MORE!

Yes ...

there's something

I MUST tell you.

This thing

I HAVE to say.

It flips my heart quite upside down
In just the nicest way.

You see ...

Whoever you are going to be ...

Whatever you may do ...

EMERGENCY
JUST-IN-CASE
PARACHUTE

Wherever you may choose to fly ...

... I'll ALWAYS love you - hoooooooo!